DATE DUE

DEC 14 1995	APR 29 1996		
JAN 17		APR 03 1998	
FEB 8			
MAY 15			
MAY 24			
OCT 03			
OCT 17			
OCT 24 1995			
JAN 17 1996			
DEC 17			
SEP 00 1997			
FEB 17 1998			
16			
NOV 24 1998			
12-08-98			

FOLLETT

STREGA NONA
Meets Her Match

written and illustrated by

Tomie dePaola

G. P. Putnam's Sons   New York

For my wonderful friend
Mary Ann Esposito
and *her* good friend
"Nellie Cucina"

G. P. Putnam's Sons, a division of The Putnam & Grosset Group,
200 Madison Avenue, New York, NY 10016.
Published simultaneously in Canada
Printed in Hong Kong by South China Printing Co. (1988) Ltd.
Type design by Werner Tomaszewski. The text is set in Veljovic.

Library of Congress Cataloging-in-Publication Data
dePaola, Tomie.   Strega Nona meets her match /
written and illustrated by Tomie dePaola.   p.   cm
Summary: A rival puts Strega Nona out of the healing business until Big Anthony's
assistance inadvertently sabotages the newcomer in his usual well-meaning way.
[1. Witches — Fiction.]   I. Title.
PZ7.D439St   1993   [E]—dc20   92-8199   CIP   AC   ISBN 0-399-22421-1

3 5 7 9 10 8 6 4

Nothing much happened in the little town in Calabria where Strega Nona lived. At least, nothing had happened since Big Anthony had left Strega Nona's magic pasta pot alone.

Bambolona, the baker's daughter, was learning how to become a *strega* too. She listened to everything Strega Nona told her. Not like Big Anthony, who never listened to anyone. Bambolona kept everything running smoothly. So life was peaceful in Strega Nona's little house on the hill.

Then one day a letter arrived for Strega Nona. It was from Strega Amelia, who lived on the other side of the mountain.

"Cara Strega Nona," the letter read. "I would like to pay you a visit. Would next week be convenient? Please let me know. *Amore e baci"*—Love and kisses—"Strega Amelia."

Strega Nona sat right down and wrote a letter telling Strega Amelia to come as soon as possible.

Big Anthony and Bambolona helped Strega Nona get the house ready. They swept and polished, and shook out the sheets.

"I have so few visitors to stay, my children," Strega Nona told them. "It will be wonderful to have company. And Big Anthony, please try to behave and pay attention while Strega Amelia is here."

"Ah, *sì*, Strega Nona," Big Anthony answered. "I'll be so good you won't recognize me!"

"I'll believe that when I see it," Bambolona whispered to Strega Nona.

"Shh. Now be nice, Bambolona," Strega Nona whispered back.

"*Ciao, cara,*" Strega Amelia called, as she reached the top of the hill.

"Ah, my dear friend," Strega Nona said. "*Avanti, avanti*"—Come in, come in.

The two *streghe* sat right down, put their heads together, and talked and laughed and gossiped until Bambolona came and stood in the doorway.

"Ah now, dear Amelia," Strega Nona said. "Bambolona has made a wonderful supper for us. *Mangia!*"—Eat!

The next morning Strega Nona was busy helping the townspeople who came to her to cure their headaches, to find husbands, and to get rid of warts.

Strega Amelia watched. "Goodness," she said to Big Anthony. "Strega Nona has *un buon numero di clienti*"—a great many customers. "Is it always this way?"

"Oh, *sì*," Big Anthony answered. "Sometimes it's even busier than this!"

"Per l'amor di Dio!"—for goodness' sake!—Strega Amelia exclaimed. "I see she still uses the old-fashioned ways too. Hmm, I'll have to think about this."

The next day Strega Amelia went home. "*Arrivederci*, Strega
Nona. Good-bye, Bambolona. Good-bye, Big Anthony," Strega
Amelia called as she went down the hill.

"*Addio*, Strega Amelia"—Farewell—the three called back.

A week later, when Big Anthony was feeding the goat, he looked out over the hillside and saw several carts coming into town. "Bambolona," he called. "Come and look."

"Why, it looks like…It is!" Bambolona said. "It's Strega Amelia. What's she up to?"

"Let's ask Strega Nona," Big Anthony said.

"No. Let's go down and find out," Bambolona said. And they crept down the hill to see for themselves.

They were back in no time.

"Strega Nona, Strega Nona," Bambolona and Big Anthony called, all out of breath.

"What is it, my children?" Strega Nona asked.

"You'll never guess. Read this!" Bambolona handed Strega Nona a handbill.

OPENING TOMORROW

STREGA AMELIA'S HELPFUL SERVICES

Husbands found for young ladies,
headaches cured,
warts removed; other remedies
Latest scientific equipment
FREE sweets and coffee with every visit

"Well," Strega Nona said. "I don't think there's anything to worry about."

But Strega Nona was wrong.

One by one the townspeople started to go to Strega Amelia.
Everyone got *dolci*—sweets—and *cappuccino* for paying a visit, and
indeed she had the latest scientific equipment—strange-looking
machines that did all kinds of things. The lines of people grew
longer and longer. Strega Nona had met her match.

Finally one morning not a single person came to Strega Nona's house. And it was that way for days and days. Poor Strega Nona!

After three weeks, Strega Nona called in Bambolona and Big Anthony.

"My children, I must talk with you. *Mia borsa*"—my purse—"is empty. I won't be able to pay you anymore. I'm afraid there is no work here. You must go down to the town and see what you can find." And Strega Nona went back into her little house.

The next morning Bambolona was there as usual. "My papa can use some help in the bakery, Strega Nona, so I'll be all right. And I'll be able to come by a few days a week to help you too!"

"Ah, my sweet Bambolona. You are so good," Strega Nona told her. "But what about our Big Anthony?"

"Here he comes now," Bambolona said.

"Oh, Strega Nona, Bambolona, you'll never guess! I have a new job!" Big Anthony shouted out, all smiles.

"You don't have to sound so happy about it." Bambolona scowled.

"Now, now," Strega Nona said. "Tell us, Big Anthony. What is it?"

"I'm going to work for Strega Amelia!" Big Anthony exclaimed.

"You're *what!*" Bambolona screamed.

"Stop! Stop!" yelled Big Anthony.

"Yes, Bambolona, stop!" Strega Nona said. "I think that is wonderful, Big Anthony. When do you start?"

"Today, Strega Nona. I have to run there right now. Wish me luck!" Big Anthony said, as he turned and ran down the hill.

"Buona fortuna"—Good luck—Strega Nona called after him.

"How could he? *How could he!* The big ungrateful traitor!" Bambolona fumed.

"Oh, Big Anthony. You are such a help to me!" Strega Amelia exclaimed, as Big Anthony followed her around doing exactly what he was told.

He polished the husband-and-wife machine.   He filled up the wart-cream jars.

He stirred the hair restorer in the big pot on the stove.

"Well, Big Anthony, business is booming," Strega Amelia remarked one morning. "I had a feeling that people would like the modern ways, especially my headache machine. And now that you have been here a few weeks, I'm going to leave you in charge for a few days while I go over the mountain to get the rest of my equipment. Now sit down and listen carefully while I explain how to run everything."

Big Anthony smiled. He was in charge.

The first day he ran the husband-and-wife machine backward.

The second day he confused the wart cream with the hair restorer.

Things weren't going too well. On the third day, the mayor arrived.

"*Buon giorno*, Signor Mayor," Big Anthony said. "What can I do for you?"

"Oh, Big Anthony," the mayor groaned. "I have a terrible headache. Strega Amelia's machine is a wonder. Strap me in."

Big Anthony settled the mayor in the headache machine and picked up the diagram that showed how to work it. He looked at the diagram. It was very complicated. (And it was upside down!)

The next morning all the townspeople were back at Strega Nona's. The mayor was the first in line.

"Bambolona," Strega Nona said, "run down and get Big Anthony. We need him."

When the carts came over the mountain with Strega Amelia in front, the townspeople were waiting at the town gate.

"I'm sorry," the mayor told Strega Amelia, "but we all agree that we prefer the old ways. Our own Strega Nona is enough for us. We hope you have no hard feelings."

"*Arrivederci*, Strega Amelia," Strega Nona said. "I'm sorry it didn't work out for you."

"*Arrivederci*, Strega Nona," Strega Amelia said. "I must admit, I am surprised. Everything was going so well. And as for your Big Anthony, I know you've had trouble with him, but I must tell you I couldn't have done it without him. He was such a big help."

"He certainly was," Strega Nona said with a smile.